Chesapeake 1 2 3

by Priscilla Cummings
illustrated by David Aiken

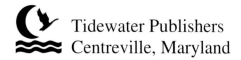

Tidewater Publishers
Centreville, Maryland

One girl went out to fish.
One pole is all she took.
One fish swam up to see . . .

But would not touch the hook!

one

Two ospreys fly up high.
Two fish they want to catch.
Two eggs are in their nest . . .

And soon those eggs will hatch.

two

Three sails are on each boat.
Three boats are in the race.
Three sailors clap and smile . . .

When their boat wins first place!

three

Four freighters on the Bay,
Four tugboats guide their way.
Four cranes wait at the port . . .

They unload crates all day.

four

Five foxes in their den,
Five possums curled up tight,
Five owls sleep on a branch . . .

They hunt all through the night.

five

Six egrets in the marsh,
Six herons in a tree,
Six geese out in the field . . .

More flying in a V!

six

With seven tiny shovels
And seven pails of sand,
Watch seven children build . . .

A castle that is grand!

seven

Eight oysters watch eight crabs.
Eight crabs are in each pot.
Eight pots on one man's boat . . .

Wow! What a lot he caught!

eight

Nine rays beneath the Bay,
Nine flounders watch them glide.
Nine turtles chase the rays . . .

And wish to have a ride.

nine

Ten cattails straight and tall,
Ten silent, sleeping bees,
Ten butterflies at rest . . .

Until there is a breeze!

ten

Let's see if you can find one fishing pole, one fish,
Two ospreys in a nest, nine turtles with a wish.
Keep searching for six geese, for three sails on a boat.
Do you see five foxes? And where four freighters float?

Now look for seven children and seven pails of sand.
Then seek out eight blue crabs, in water and on land.
Ten butterflies are hiding in bushes where there's shade.
Now find nine rays down deep,
                              and see the friends they've made.

By now you know those numbers.
Let's hear them once again.
1, 2, 3, 4, 5–Chesapeake!
Then 6, 7, 8, 9, 10!